First printing, 2021 Kindle Direct Publishing
ISBN 978-1-7373150-0-1
A Grandma Hug
Southerngyrl Publishing, LLC.
Dallas, TX
southernauthor2@gmail.com

Illustration and Layout Design
Julie Anderson
kidart@mac.com

Printed in the United States of America

In honor of my Mother, Catherine Hall Williams, for the life lesson of lavishing merciful love to the children of our communities with something as simple as a grandmother's hug.

A Grandma Hug

Written by Bailey Wynne   Illustrated by Julie Anderson

It happened on the way to bed
That PJ fell and hit his head.

Loudly crying
with lots of tears,
wailed mommy, mommy
I need you here!

Up the stairs
she flew to see,
what is the
matter,
my sweet pea?

She picked him up
and held him
close,
rubbed his
back,
then wiped
his nose.

I bumped my head
and there's a knot.
Right there,
right there,
it hurts a lot.

I'll kiss it sweetie. Now it is fine.
Now off to sleep little boy of mine.

Dad's gone to work some time ago.
He gave you smooches then you know.

Now close your eyes and go to sleep.
Not a sound now.
Not a peep.

No mommy, no, my eyes are sad.
I need a grandma hug real bad!

When Grandma's here, she hugs me tight,
and tells me that I'll be alright.

I need her hug, please pretty please.
Call her to bring my hug, a squeeze.

Ding Dong!
Who's at the door? It's very late.
Why grandma, it is after eight.

But PJ's up and says he needs
your very special grandma squeeze.

Grandma, grandma, I hit my head,
While I was getting into bed.

Look, look. See it? See that knot.
All big up there, right there on top.

Come little one, your grandma's here
to make the sadness disappear.

I've got a hug here just for you.
You'll be alright, I know it's true.

Now, into bed and go to sleep.
Let me kiss those precious cheeks.

One extra hug, now close your eyes.
Sweet dreams, my little sweetie pie.

Goodnight grandma, I'm really glad
you brought to me, my hug you had.

My eyes are happy,
that knot is
down.
My mouth
no longer
has a
frown.

And,
with a smile
upon his face,
he yawned
and got
a last
embrace.

Then closing his eyes,
no longer sad,
PJ fell asleep,
a happy lad.

Bailey Wynne

Bailey is a noter of life's notables, a mom, daughter, sister, aunt, wife, clinical pharmacist and happily, a doting grandmother. She writes poetry, fiction and childrens' books that encourage authentic living, a zest for adventures, the wonder of science and random acts of kindness.

southernauthor2@gmail.com   boomertales.website

Julie Anderson

A Normal, IL native, Julie began her lifelong love of drawing as soon as she could hold a pencil. She has illustrated many books and instructional materials for young children. She now calls Cary, NC home with her husband, two grown sons and two sweet pups.

kidart@mac.com   facebook.com/julieandersonillustration/

Made in United States
North Haven, CT
05 July 2022